R0055707467

06/2011

W9-BBT-610

OLIVIA™
Goes Camping

adapted by Alex Harvey
based on the screenplay written by Patrick Resnick
illustrated by Jared Osterhold

Ready-to-Read

Simon Spotlight

New York   London   Toronto   Sydney

Based on the TV series *OLIVIA*™ as seen on Nickelodeon™

SIMON SPOTLIGHT
An imprint of Simon & Schuster Children's Publishing Division
1230 Avenue of the Americas, New York, New York 10020
Copyright © 2011 Silver Lining Productions Limited (a Chorion company). All rights reserved.
OLIVIA™ and © 2011 Ian Falconer. All rights reserved.
All rights reserved, including the right of reproduction in whole or in part in any form.
SIMON SPOTLIGHT, READY-TO-READ, and colophon are registered trademarks of Simon & Schuster, Inc.
For information about special discounts for bulk purchases,
please contact Simon & Schuster Special Sales at 1-866-506-1949 or business@simonandschuster.com.
Manufactured in the United States of America 0511 LAK
First Edition
2 4 6 8 10 9 7 5 3 1
ISBN 978-1-4424-2253-7 (hc)
ISBN 978-1-4424-2135-6 (pbk)

Olivia and her family
are going camping.

Olivia's best friend,
Francine, is going too.

Francine does not think
she likes camping.
"I will get dirty and wet,"
she says.

"Camping is fun," Olivia tells her.
"There are five things you must do on a great camping trip."

"Number one: watch my dad try to put up the tent."

"He will forget to put in all the poles.

And the tent will fall

down!"

"Dad always needs my help," Olivia says.

Olivia tells Francine to use
the hammer to bang the
tent stake into the ground.

"Now, the number two thing is to climb a mountain."

"But my foot hurts,"
Francine says.

"Do you want to lie down?"
Olivia asks.
"I will get dirty if I lie
down," says Francine.
Olivia says that getting
dirty is part of camping.

It is number three on her list.

"But I don't want to get dirty," Francine says.

Francine brought her blanket, pillow, and cot. Olivia brought her sleeping bag.

Number four on Olivia's list: find a really cool bug.

"Ow! I got bitten by a mosquito," Francine says.

"That doesn't count," says Olivia.

"But it itches," Francine says.

"Mud is great for bug bites," Olivia says.

"Eww! I am dirty and wet
and covered with mud!"
Francine cries.
"I need a shower!"

Olivia ties a bag of water
to a tree branch.
Then she pokes holes
in the bag.

Olivia tells Francine that
number five on the list
is to find a perfect stick
to roast marshmallows.

"One end of the stick
must be sharp," says Olivia.
"But not too sharp!"

"This stick has too many branches.

This one is too long . . .

and this one is too short."

"How about this one?"
Francine asks.

"Perfect!" says Olivia.
"You are a great camper,
Francine."